"Let me out!"

Lucy looked around h anywhere near. The voic coming out of the bottle Lucy, a bit nervously.

"Let me *out!*" repeated the voice, only this time a little hysterically. "I'm in the bottle. Over here ... that's right!"

When Lucy lets the genie out of the bottle, she sets off a stream of funny, unpredictable events for her family and, most of all, for Mitch, their dog. A very amusing story, ideal for building reading confidence.

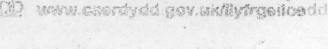

YOUNG CORGI BOOKS

Young Corgi books are perfect when you are looking for great books to read on your own. They are full of exciting stories and entertaining pictures and can be tackled with confidence. There are funny books, scary books, spine-tingling stories and mysterious ones. Whatever your interests you'll find something in Young Corgi to suit you: from ponies to football, from families to ghosts. The books are written by some of the most famous and popular of today's children's authors, and by some of the best new talents, too.

Whether you read one chapter a night, or devour the whole book in one sitting, you'll love Young Corgi books. The more you read, the more you'll want to read!

Other Young Corgi books to get your teeth into

BLACK QUEEN by Michael Morpurgo

LIZZIE ZIPMOUTH by Jacqueline Wilson

SAMMY'S SUPER SEASON
by Lindsay Camp

ANIMAL CRACKERS by Narinder Dhami

DOG MAGIC!

To my mum and dad

DOG MAGIC!
A YOUNG CORGI BOOK : 978 0 552 57189 0

PRINTING HISTORY
Young Corgi edition published 2000

3 5 7 9 10 8 6 4

Set in 17/21pt Bembo Schoolbook

Young Corgi Books are published by Random House Children's Books,
61–63 Uxbridge Road, London W5 5SA,
a division of The Random House Group Ltd.

The Random House Group Limited supports The Forest Stewardship
Council® (FSC®), the leading international forest-certification organisation.
Our books carrying the FSC label are printed on FSC®-certified paper.
FSC is the only forest-certification scheme supported by the leading
environmental organisations, including Greenpeace. Our
paper procurement policy can be found at
www.randomhouse.co.uk/environment

MIX
Paper from
responsible sources
FSC www.fsc.org FSC® C018072

Printed and bound in Great Britain by Clays Ltd, St Ives plc

DOG MAGIC!

Written and illustrated by
Chris Priestley

YOUNG CORGI

DOG MAGIC!

Written and Illustrated by
Chris Powling

YOUNG CORGI

Chapter One

The Genie in the Bottle Bank

"What is the matter with you, Lucy? You've been moping around all day."

"I'm bored," said Lucy, flopping back into an armchair. "Everything's so . . . so . . ."

"Boring?" asked her mother, smiling.

"Yes," laughed Lucy. "Boring, boring, boring."

"Oh, dear," said her mother, "and the school holidays only started last week. Why don't you go for a ride on your bike?"

"Don't want to," said Lucy.

"OK," said her mother, starting to frown. "How about doing the homework you were set?"

"Done it," said Lucy. Her mother scowled.

"Why don't you just watch TV, then, for goodness sake!"

"Nothing on," said Lucy.

"Grrr," said her mother, grabbing Lucy by the arm and pulling her to her feet. "Then you can come and help me take some rubbish to the dump."

"Oh, Mum," moaned Lucy.

"Never mind 'Oh, Mum', come and help me with these empty bottles –

and get Mitch and we'll take him for a walk afterwards. You could do with some exercise, you lazy lump!"

"Oh," said Lucy, making a fuss of her dog, "what's she saying? You're not a lazy lump, are you, Mitch?"

"I wasn't talking about Mitch," said her mother.

★

The dump was only a short drive away from where they lived; it was tucked away, out of sight, behind a petrol station. It was surrounded by a high chicken-wire fence and was full of skips, each with a different sign on it, saying things like GENERAL WASTE, CARDBOARD RECYCLING and GREEN WASTE ONLY, where Lucy's mother put the bits she pruned from her rose bushes.

Around the skips were all sorts of
things that people had brought to
throw away: broken bicycles, old
cookers and rusty machinery, and
inside one of the skips there was
sometimes a man sorting through all
the rubbish. You had to be careful to
look before you threw your rubbish
in, in case you hit him on the head.

There were two other huge containers at the dump, one for newspapers and another for empty bottles. The one for bottles was called a bottle bank and once, when Lucy's mum had asked her dad what he was taking to the dump, he said, "Some bottles for the bottle bank and some piggies for the piggy bank." He was always cracking terrible jokes, Lucy's dad.

"Can I do the bottles, Mum?" asked Lucy when they got out of the car.

"OK," said her mother, "anything to keep you quiet. But be careful. I don't want any dropped. I'll go and do the papers. Shut up, Mitch!" Mitch was barking in the back of the car. He always barked at the dump. No-one really knew why, but Lucy's Dad said it was because all Jack Russell terriers were bonkers.

There was a little metal platform by the bottle bank so that even if you were not very tall, you could still reach the holes to put your bottles in. Lucy climbed the steps and took the first of her bottles out of her carrier bag, but just as she was about to post it through the hole she heard a voice. "Let me out!"

Lucy looked around her. There was no-one anywhere near. The voice seemed to be coming out of the bottle bank!

"Hello?" said Lucy, a bit nervously.

"Let me *out!*" repeated the voice, only this time a little hysterically. "I'm in the bottle. Over here . . . that's right!" The voice was coming from a strange-looking bottle with a long twisted neck and a glass stopper, which was sticking out from one of the holes.

Lucy pulled at the bottle and the stopper came out with a loud *POP*. Lucy stumbled backwards dropping all the bottles with a great *SMASH* on the ground.

"Lucy!" yelled her mother.

"Oh, no!" groaned Lucy. Her mother came rushing over.

"What did I tell you? Do I have to do everything myself? Look at all this . . ."

"Mess" is what Lucy's mother was going to say, but she never finished the sentence and stood there stock still, staring over Lucy's shoulder.

Baffled, Lucy turned round to see what it was her mum was looking at. To her amazement she saw that a huge man, the height of a double-decker bus, was emerging from a cloud of smoke billowing up from the bottle that she had opened.

"That's better," he said, stretching. "And this must be the clever little girl who set me free."

"Wh . . . wh . . . who are you?" said Lucy nervously.

"Why, I'm a genie, my child, and as a reward for setting me free from that horrible bottle, I have the power to grant three wishes."

"Wow!" said Lucy's mother.

"Cool!" said Lucy, but then almost immediately said, "Why only three wishes?"

"Well, I don't know," said the genie. "It's traditional."

"You could have been trapped in
that bottle for ever, if it hadn't been
for me," said Lucy.

"Lucy!" said her mother angrily. "Will you *stop* being so greedy?"

But the genie laughed a great booming laugh. "No, no, no. Lucy is right. How about if I give you unlimited wishes for, say, one year?"

"Oh, yes please! That's much better," said Lucy.

"OK then," said the genie, and he waved his huge arms around and then pointed towards Lucy. A strange glittery beam began to move in Lucy's direction. Just then, Mitch, who had grown very bored in the car and had wriggled through a half open window, came bounding over. He leapt in between Lucy and the genie, who promptly disappeared.

"Sorry," said the genie's voice, trailing away into the distance. "Hate dogs. Good luck. See you in a year."

"Wow!" said Lucy, thinking about

how great it would be if there were a
Disneyworld in the local park.

"Come on," said Lucy's mum (who
was already thinking about the new
kitchen she would have, not to
mention the holiday in the
Bahamas). "Let's go home and think
very carefully about what we really
want to wish for."

Chapter Two

Dinosaur Bones in the Kitchen

All the way back from the dump, Lucy and her mum thought about all the things they would wish for. The list was endless. They could have anything they wanted – anything at all. Life, thought Lucy, will never be boring again.

They ran into the house with Mitch bounding after them. Lucy's father was just coming in from doing some gardening.

"Slow down!" said Lucy's dad. "You seem very excited about something."

"Dad! Dad!" shouted Lucy, jumping up and down. "We've been to the dump!"

"Well, you'll have to go more often

as you seem to enjoy it so much,"
said her dad, laughing.

"No, Jim," said Lucy's mum. "You
don't understand. There was a genie
and he's given us unlimited wishes for
a year!"

"Oh," said her father, winking, "I *see*."

"It's true, Dad. Honest!" said Lucy. "I rescued him from a bottle in the bottle bank and he was huge and he said I could have three wishes and I said 'Why only three?' and so he said he'd give me all the wishes I want for a whole year!"

"That does sound like you, I must say," said her father, smiling.

"So you believe us then?" said Lucy's mum.

"Of course I don't believe you! Come on, a joke's a joke, but really."

"Look, Jim," said her mum, getting cross, "I know it sounds incredible, but Lucy's telling the truth. There's no mistake. You should have seen him – he was the size of a house and then he just disappeared into thin air."

"OK then," said Lucy's father with

a sigh, "why hasn't anything changed?"

"We haven't wished for anything yet," snapped Lucy's mother.

"I'm sorry, but I can't believe that Lucy has resisted the temptation to wish for something all the way home from the dump. If Lucy could wish for anything she wanted we'd have Disneyworld in the back garden by now," said her dad, sounding a little cross.

This had worried Lucy herself. She had not been able to stop herself wishing for something, just to test to see if it worked, and so she had wished for Mitch to turn into a pony, but nothing had happened. It was probably just as well as it would have been a bit of a tight squeeze in the back of the car.

She had decided that she must need a bit more practice and so she thought she would wish for something smaller. This time she wished for the shoes she had seen in the shop window in town, which her mum had said were too expensive. Again, nothing.

"Maybe you have to say it out loud," said Lucy, "or it doesn't count."

"Well, OK then," said her father, folding his arms. "Let's hear you wish for something."

"Yes, Lucy," said her mum, "wish

for something. Go on."

"What shall I wish for?" said Lucy, her mind suddenly a blank.

"Well, I could do with a new pair of slippers," said her dad, wiggling his toes inside his socks.

"Right, then," said Lucy, "here goes. I wish that Dad had some new slippers."

Everyone looked at Lucy's father's feet. They were completely slipperless.

"Finished now? A genie in the bottle bank? Good grief!"

"It's not fair!" shouted Lucy. "He promised. He promised! He prom. . ."

Just then there was a very loud crash, as if one of those huge dinosaur skeletons you see in museums had fallen from a great height onto the kitchen floor. The whole family rushed to the kitchen and there, piled high on the floor and on the table and on the work surfaces, were the huge bones from a dinosaur skeleton!

"What the . . .?" said Lucy's dad.

"I didn't wish for that," said Lucy, and Mitch sauntered in looking very pleased with himself.

"Oh no," said Lucy's mum. "You know when the genie pointed to you and Mitch jumped up at him?"

"You don't mean to say that . . ." began her dad.

"MITCH HAS GOT MY WISHES!" yelled Lucy.

Chapter Three

Talking Terrier

The magic beam from the genie's fingers had hit Mitch, not Lucy, and it was Mitch, not Lucy, who had unlimited wishes for a year.

"You stupid dog," said Lucy's father. "You could wish for anything in the whole world and you wish for a load of old bones."

"Be fair, darling, they are *dinosaur* bones," said Lucy's mum, and then she whispered, "I'm not sure it's wise to call Mitch 'stupid' when he's got magic powers. He's not very keen on you at the best of times."

"Good point," said Lucy's dad, eyeing Mitch nervously. "Sorry, Mitch, old boy. Only kidding."

He went to pat Mitch on the head but Mitch only growled at him.

"Perhaps, if we're extra-specially nice to him," said Lucy's mum, tickling Mitch behind the ear, "Mitch might wish for something for us, mightn't you, boy, eh? Like a lovely new kitchen, for instance . . . Or a new house, even."

"Yeah," said Lucy, warming to this idea, "if we were *really* nice to him, he might wish that there was a Disneyworld just round the corner."

"If I let the little rascal chew my shoes, he might even see his way to wishing me a new car," said Lucy's father, a little hopefully. "What do you say, little fellow? Any chance?"

"I suppose there is *some* chance," said Mitch half-heartedly, "but I feel it's only fair to warn you that it's a very *slim* chance."

"Why you cheeky . . ." began Lucy's dad. "Wait a minute! Did you hear what I heard?"

"Mitch can talk!" said all three of them in astonishment.

"I thought it might be helpful," said Mitch, "you know, communication-wise."

"Yes," said Lucy's mum, "I suppose it will."

"I must admit I didn't expect you to sound quite so, well, you know . . ." said Lucy's dad, getting flustered.

"Intelligent?" suggested Mitch.

"You do sound very clever, Mitch," said Lucy.

"There's no need to sound quite so surprised."

"Sorry," said Lucy.

"That's OK," said Mitch, "you're only human. Anyway, having you guess what I wanted was getting very tiresome. Take the other day, for instance. It was perfectly obvious that I wanted some water but oh, no," said Mitch, looking at Lucy's father, "that was far too difficult for him to work out, so he decided I wanted to go outside instead, and chucked me out in the pouring rain. I was soaked through."

Lucy's dad tried very hard not to snigger, but unfortunately for him, not hard enough. There was a crack of thunder and suddenly rain was lashing against the windows.

"Oh," said Mitch, "you think it's amusing, do you?" Before Lucy's father could answer, he disappeared from the living room and reappeared out in the garden tied to the post that held the washing line, getting soaked to the skin in the torrential rain.

"Bring him in out of the rain, Mitch. He's very sorry," said Lucy's mum. "You're very sorry, aren't you?" she shouted through the window at her husband.

"Yes," growled Lucy's dad. "I'
sorry."

"He doesn't *sound*
very sorry," said
Mitch, settling
himself on the sofa,
and the rain turned
to snow.

"No, he really is –
aren't you, Dad?"
called Lucy.

"Y . . . Y . . . Y . . .
Yes," shivered Lucy's
dad. "R . . . R . . . R . . . Really
sorry."

"Are you sure?" said Mitch.

"YES!" shouted Lucy's father.

"Well, OK then," said Mitch, and
Lucy's dad reappeared in the living
room, shaking with cold and
beginning to turn a little blue.

"It's f . . . f . . . freezing out there."

"Oh, you are making a fuss," said Mitch, "it looks fine to me," and sure enough, when they looked outside, the snow and rain had stopped and the sun was shining out of a bright blue sky.

Everyone realized that they were going to have to be very careful how they spoke to Mitch. He was clearly enjoying his new-found powers. They all wondered what he was going to wish for next.

"You're all wondering what I'm going to wish for next, aren't you?" said Mitch, closing his eyes and yawning. "And yet you haven't even noticed my first wish."

Mitch fell asleep, exhausted by all the excitement. Lucy and her mum and dad looked at each other and shrugged there shoulders. What on earth could Mitch's first wish have been?

Chapter Four

Vanishing Cats

The next day, Mrs O'Henry from number 35 knocked on the door and asked if Lucy's mother had seen Hugo, her cat. Lucy's mum said that she had not seen Hugo all day, but if she did she would be sure to tell her.

"Poor Mrs O'Henry," said Lucy's mother. "She dotes on that cat."

"Pah!" said Mitch. "I will never understand the strange attraction you humans have towards those awful animals. We'd all be better off without them if you ask me."

"You've got a point there, Mitch," said Lucy's dad, who, as it happened, really did agree with Mitch on this occasion because Hugo and the other cats in the neighbourhood were forever climbing into the garden and using his vegetable patch as a toilet.

"Still," said Lucy's mum, "Mrs O'Henry looked very worried."

Mitch climbed slowly out of his dog basket, yawned and said, "Why would anyone in their right minds choose to give houseroom to a cat, when they could, instead, give a home to man's *best* friend, the dog?"

"When you put it like that," said Lucy, "it does seem strange." Secretly she was thinking what a terrible big-head Mitch had become.

"You see," said Lucy's mum, "Mrs O'Henry's children are all grown up and have left home, so she's only got Hugo to make a fuss over."

"Do you mean to say she thinks of that fluffy flea-ridden feline as a *child*?" asked Mitch.

"Well, sort of," said Lucy's mother, beginning to wish she had never started.

"And so, if Hugo were to, say, disappear, then she would *miss* him?" said Mitch incredulously.

"Well, of course she would, Mitch," said Lucy.

"Extraordinary!" said Mitch. "Still, Mrs O'Henry has always been very nice to me and so we'll have to see what we can do to help."

"Oh, Mitch," said Lucy, smiling. "Are you going to wish for Mrs O'Henry to get Hugo back?"

"No, no," said Mitch, "I think we can do a little better than that."

A little later a terrible commotion erupted in the street. Lucy's dad went to the window. "It's Mrs O'Henry," he said, "and there's a crowd of people outside her house. What exactly have you done, Mitch?"

"Oh, you'll see," he said, smugly.

They got to Mrs O'Henry's house just as the police arrived. "What's going on, Mrs O?" asked Lucy's father.

"They just appeared. I came into the lounge with a nice cup of tea and a chocolate biscuit, all ready to watch my favourite quiz show, and there they were!"

"What were?" asked Lucy.

"Why, the children, of course — four boys, about five years old, quads, by the look of them. I mean, how did they get there?"

"Mitch!" said Lucy.

"What was that?" said the policewoman who had just appeared on the doorstep. "Do any of you have any information concerning this incident?"

"No, officer," they said, which was not strictly true, but how could they tell the police that their Jack Russell terrier had wished the children on Mrs O'Henry as a replacement for her missing cat?

"Then could I ask you to please leave and let the police handle this. I'm sure there is a perfectly sensible explanation," said the policewoman bossily.

They went home and found Mitch dozing in his basket. "I suppose you think you're very clever," said Lucy's mother.

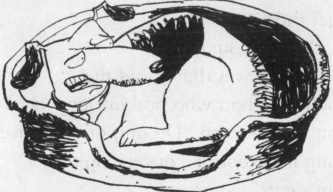

Mitch blinked a couple of times and yawned. "Is there some problem?" he said absent-mindedly.

"Mrs O'Henry, Mitch . . . and those four little children," said Lucy.

"She must be delighted," said Mitch. "Now she'll forget all about that silly cat."

"But she's sixty-four, Mitch," said Lucy's mum. "She's too old to look after four children, and anyway no-one but us knows how the children got there. They'll probably arrest her."

"That's the trouble with you humans, you're always complaining," said Mitch angrily. "I try and help, out of the goodness of my heart, and you're still not satisfied."

"What are we going to do?" said Lucy's mother, once they were outside and out of earshot.

"I don't know," said Lucy's father, "but this is getting out of hand. There's no telling what he'll wish for next."

"Which reminds me," said Lucy, "we never did find out what Mitch's first ever wish was."

"That's right," said Lucy's mum. "Still, it can't have been a very big wish, or we would have noticed something."

"*I've* noticed something," said Lucy.

"What's that, sweetheart?" said her dad.

"It's not just Hugo that's missing. *All* the cats have gone!"

They looked around and sure enough, there was not a single cat to be seen and old Mr Singh was whistling forlornly on his step and shaking a packet of cat biscuits. There were normally lots of cats in the neighbourhood, but now the whole area was deserted.

"Mitch!" they all said at once.

"I wonder what the little monster's done with them all," said Lucy's dad.

"You don't think he's . . ." began her mum.

"What?" asked Lucy.

"You know," said her mum.

"*What?*" said Lucy again, but her mum and dad just stood looking very seriously at each other.

"What have you done with them, just out of interest," Lucy's dad asked Mitch, when they went back inside.

"With what? Oh, the cats. Is there a problem? I certainly hope none of you are sticking up for those disgusting creatures."

"No, no!" said Lucy's dad.

"Not me," said Lucy.

"Nor me," said her mum.

"Jolly good," said Mitch, "then we'll say no more about it."

They found out what had happened eventually. That evening on the news, the newsreader smiled and said, "And finally . . . They have been having some terrible weather on the tiny Scottish island of Inch Macmoodle. It has been raining cats and dogs . . . Well, it's been raining cats, anyway! The puzzled population of Inch Macmoodle awoke this morning to find dozens of cats had appeared from nowhere . . ."

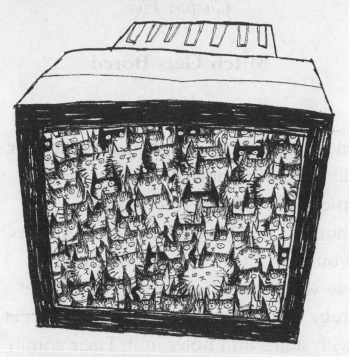

"Wait a minute," said Lucy's dad, "that ginger tom in the front. That's Mrs O'Henry's cat, isn't it?"

"Hugo!" said Lucy and her mother. And so it was. Mitch had sent all the cats in the neighbourhood to Scotland!

"They won't bother me up there," laughed Mitch.

Chapter Five

Mitch Gets Bored

In the following days Mitch wished for all kinds of things. He wished for smelly old slippers to chew, even though Lucy thought her dad's slippers would be smelly enough for anyone. He wished for their lovely new carpet to be replaced by a revolting old carpet with stains and holes in it. Their comfy chairs disappeared and Mitch wished up a horrible armchair that looked and smelled like it had come from the dump.

Mitch insisted on having his friends round all the time and the house was filled with yelping, yapping and slobbering dogs. They would bound around the house getting in everyone's

way and eat any food that wasn't
locked up. They would bark and fight
all day and then squabble and howl all
night. Nobody got a wink of sleep.

And bones! There were bones
everywhere, every size and shape
imaginable. Lucy and her parents were

forever tripping over them or finding them down the back of the sofa or under the carpet, or even in their *beds*! It was disgusting.

Then one morning Lucy looked out of her bedroom window to find an enormous kennel, painted bright red and bigger than their house. It sat right on top of her dad's vegetable patch and you could see a couple of squashed cabbage plants sticking out

from under it. Mitch told them that he was finding his kennel a bit cramped for his liking, so he had wished for a new one. It was centrally heated and he had a fluffy rug to lie on and a tatty old basket to sleep in. It was really rather cosy, despite its size.

Walks with Mitch took on a whole new dimension now he had magical powers. He announced one day that the walk around the park, along the river and home again was far too boring and so now, when Lucy took Mitch out he wished them to a different location each time. It would have been fun if Mitch had not become so full of himself.

Sometimes Mitch would wish them to the countryside so that he could chase rabbits down their burrows or run through the woods sniffing all the trees. He would roll around in the fields

where the cows had been. Sometimes
they would go to the seaside and
Mitch would bark at the sea and dig
holes in the sand.

Whatever he did, he
would always come back smellier than
ever – and he absolutely refused to
have a bath.

Lucy thought how funny it was that
even with all his unlimited wishes, the
thing Mitch enjoyed most was having
a stick thrown for him to go and fetch.

Mitch didn't have to wish for *that* at all, he and Lucy played that game every time they went to the park. Or they used to, anyway.

So it went on, until gradually Lucy noticed that Mitch was wishing for fewer and fewer of their walks and eating more and more doggy chocolates. His friends still clattered around the house but, more and more, Mitch was to be found alone in the huge kennel sitting in his basket. And he was getting fat.

Mitch seemed tired all the time and often snoozed all day long. The only thing he wished for now was food and most of the time he didn't even eat it. It was as if he couldn't think of anything else to wish for. He hardly ever talked and if you didn't know how special he was, you would think he was just a spoilt and very lazy dog.

When he and Lucy did go on a walk, Mitch would often lag behind and Lucy would have to wait for him to catch up. He stopped chasing rabbits and when they went to the beach he just lay about sunbathing. He certainly wasn't his old self.

"Where are we going today, Mitch?" said Lucy, walking into Mitch's kennel one day.

"Oh, I'm not sure I want to go anywhere to be honest, Lucy," replied Mitch with a yawn. "It's all so . . . so . . . well, *boring*."

"Boring?" said Lucy, "But you can go anywhere you want, do whatever you want."

"I know, I know," said Mitch, "but it's *still* boring. I think I'll have a snooze instead."

"A snooze?" said Lucy. "A *snooze*? You're always snoozing, these days. You can wish for *anything*! How can you be bored?"

"I know," said Mitch, "it does seem impossible, doesn't it? But I assure you I am. Bored, that is. Very bored. Now, if you'll excuse me, I'm going to have that snooze. Bye. You can see yourself out, can't you? Thanks for dropping by. Catch you later. . ."

Lucy walked back to the house and

went to her bedroom. One of Mitch's friends was asleep on her bed and growled when she tried to shoo him off, so she sat on the stairs outside the bathroom. She was feeling very sorry for herself. Her mother came out and sat next to her, giving her a cuddle.

"Not taking Mitch for a walk?" said her mum.

"Mitch says he's bored," said Lucy.

"He certainly doesn't seem very happy," said her mum.

"But that's crazy. He's got everything he wants," sobbed Lucy.

"Maybe," said her mum, "having everything you want isn't all it's cracked up to be."

"Hmm," said Lucy and she tried to think how that could *possibly* be true.

Chapter Six

The Genie Returns

Lucy thought about what her mum
had said about Mitch being unhappy
and she decided to go and see him.
Lucy was the only one who visited
Mitch now, though she often wondered
why she bothered because he wasn't
really very good company. Each time
she visited she noticed the kennel
getting shabbier and shabbier and
smellier and smellier. There were half-
eaten biscuits and slightly gnawed
bones all over the place. It really was
quite disgusting.

Lucy found Mitch looking particularly miserable. "Hello, Mitch," she said. "How about a walk? We could go to the beach. You could do with a bit of exercise!"

"Sorry, Lucy, I just can't face going for a walk today. Think I'll just hang around the kennel and, well, you know . . ."

"Snooze," said Lucy, frowning. "Oh, Mitch. You used to be so full of fun. Now look at you. You've turned into a . . . a . . ."

"Yes?" said Mitch, lifting one ear and frowning.

"Into a lazy lump!" blurted Lucy, instantly regretting it. She closed her eyes and waited. But nothing happened. She peeped cautiously out of one eye, but instead of being angry, Mitch had his head between his paws and was sobbing.

"It's true," he wailed. "I *am* a lazy lump! A great big fat lazy lump!" And he wailed even louder.

"There, there, Mitch. Don't cry."

"But everybody *hates* me!" blubbed Mitch.

"No, no, of course they don't," said Lucy, trying to sound convincing.

"Yes, they do. Nobody loves me!" And he sobbed and blubbed and wailed.

Lucy tickled him behind the ear the way she used to when he was just an ordinary dog and slowly, very slowly, Mitch's tail began to wag.

"Tell me, Lucy," he said when he'd calmed down a little, "*do* people hate me?"

"Oh, I wouldn't say 'hate'," said Lucy, "but you have been pretty horrible, you know."

"Do you know what?" said Mitch. "I wish that genie were here now, so that I could tell him what to do with all his wishes!"

"And what's that?" said a booming voice and they turned round to see the genie's smiling face at the open door of the kennel. He was far too big to get into even Mitch's enormous kennel.

"I . . . I . . . I . . ." stammered Mitch.

"Come on now. Spit it out," said the genie.

"I don't want these wishes," said Mitch.

"Don't want them?" said the genie. "Are you sure?"

"Positive," said Mitch, "and anyway, they weren't even *my* wishes. It was Lucy you really meant to give the wishes to, wasn't it?"

"Well, I don't want them either," said Lucy. "Not after seeing what happened to Mitch."

"Very well," agreed the genie. He turned to Mitch. "If you don't want the wishes then I'll take them back, but why not have one last wish before I do? What is the one thing you would like more than anything else in the whole world?"

"For everything to be like it was before," cried Mitch. And so it was. In a flash, the giant kennel was gone and they were standing in the middle of the vegetable patch.

"Hey, mind my runner beans," said
Lucy's father, running out of the house
and then skidding to a sudden stop.
"G . . . G . . . Good grief! Y . . . Y . . .
You must be the genie."

"Pleased to meet you," said the genie.
"Sorry about the beans."

"Wait a minute. Where's the kennel?"
asked Lucy's mother when she appeared.

"Mitch wished it all away. He wanted things to be the way they were. And so did I," said Lucy.

"Even though it gets boring sometimes?" said Lucy's mum, giving her a hug.

"Sorry I was so greedy, Mr Genie," said Lucy.

"Oh, no," said the Genie, "I haven't had this much fun in ages. Well, I'll say goodbye, then. Thanks again for letting me out of the bottle . . ." And he was gone.

"Bye!" they all shouted. All that is except Mitch, who could no longer talk and just had to bark, but who looked much happier. They all stared into the distance at the place where he disappeared until Lucy's mum said, "Who's for a nice cup of tea?"

"Great idea," said Lucy's dad, following her indoors.

"Well, Mitch," said Lucy, "I'm glad all that's over. I'm sorry I called you a fat lump." But Mitch was not really listening. He suddenly bounded off into the house as fast as his little legs would carry him.

"It looks like everything's back to normal," said Lucy to herself, and she went indoors to watch TV.

But just as she stepped through the front door she heard a terrible commotion coming from the lounge. She peeped nervously round the door . . . All the neighbourhood cats had reappeared – in Lucy's house! Mitch was going crazy chasing them round the furniture and up the curtains. A couple of the cats had even decided to jump up onto Lucy's dad's head for safety and he was shouting and trying to get them off, while her mum tried to shoo the others out with a broom.

Maybe I'll play outside today, thought Lucy, with a giggle. And that's exactly what she did.

THE END